LUDWIG THE SPACE DOG

To Linus Ludwig –
I wish you a life full of discoveries.

A TEMPLAR BOOK

First published in the UK in 2016 by Templar Publishing,
part of the Bonnier Publishing Group,
The Plaza, 535 King's Road, London, SW10 0SZ
www.templarco.co.uk
www.bonnierpublishing.com

Text and illustration copyright © 2016 by Henning Löhlein
Design copyright © 2016 by The Templar Company Limited

1 3 5 7 9 10 8 6 4 2
0716 008

ISBN 978-1-78370-389-0

Designed by Genevieve Webster
Edited by Katie Haworth

Printed in China

LUDWIG
THE SPACE DOG

Henning Löhlein

templar publishing

Petula loved flowers.

Jackson was the smallest.

Mack loved green.

Ludwig and his friends lived
in a world of books.

Ludwig was
very curious.

Sophie was
super strong.

Enzo loved
playing ball
and bouncing.

The six friends loved to play all through the pages of their world.

But Ludwig also loved to read. His favourite books were about flying in space.

Every night, Ludwig dreamed
of zooming past cheese moons
and sausage planets.
He always woke up hungry
in the morning.

His friends tried to help him too,
but nothing seemed to work.

Then Ludwig read a book about birds and had a brilliant idea.

He tied feathers to his arms and flapped and flapped . . .

BANG

Ludwig realised there was only one thing to do – he would have to build something to help him fly.

He stayed up all night reading books about it.

The next day, Ludwig and his friends built a plane.

Things started well . . .

Ludwig was running out of ideas.

Maybe he'd never fly.

Ludwig looked at the rocket's engine.
He'd read all about them, so he knew
exactly what to do.

While Ludwig and his friends were busy, the space explorer looked at all the books and paper.

And once Ludwig had explained the engine problem . . .

. . . they all set to work.

Enzo jumped to the top of the rocket.

Petula did some cosmetic repairs.

I LIKE PINK.

Sophie lifted the rocket . . .

. . . and Jackson climbed into the smallest corner to fix a fuel pipe.

The space explorer asked
everyone to come along.

THANK YOU
SO MUCH, YOU ARE
A GREAT TEAM! WOULD
YOU LIKE TO COME
EXPLORING THE WORLD
WITH ME?

Ludwig's friends said they didn't have time, but
Ludwig hopped into the rocket ...

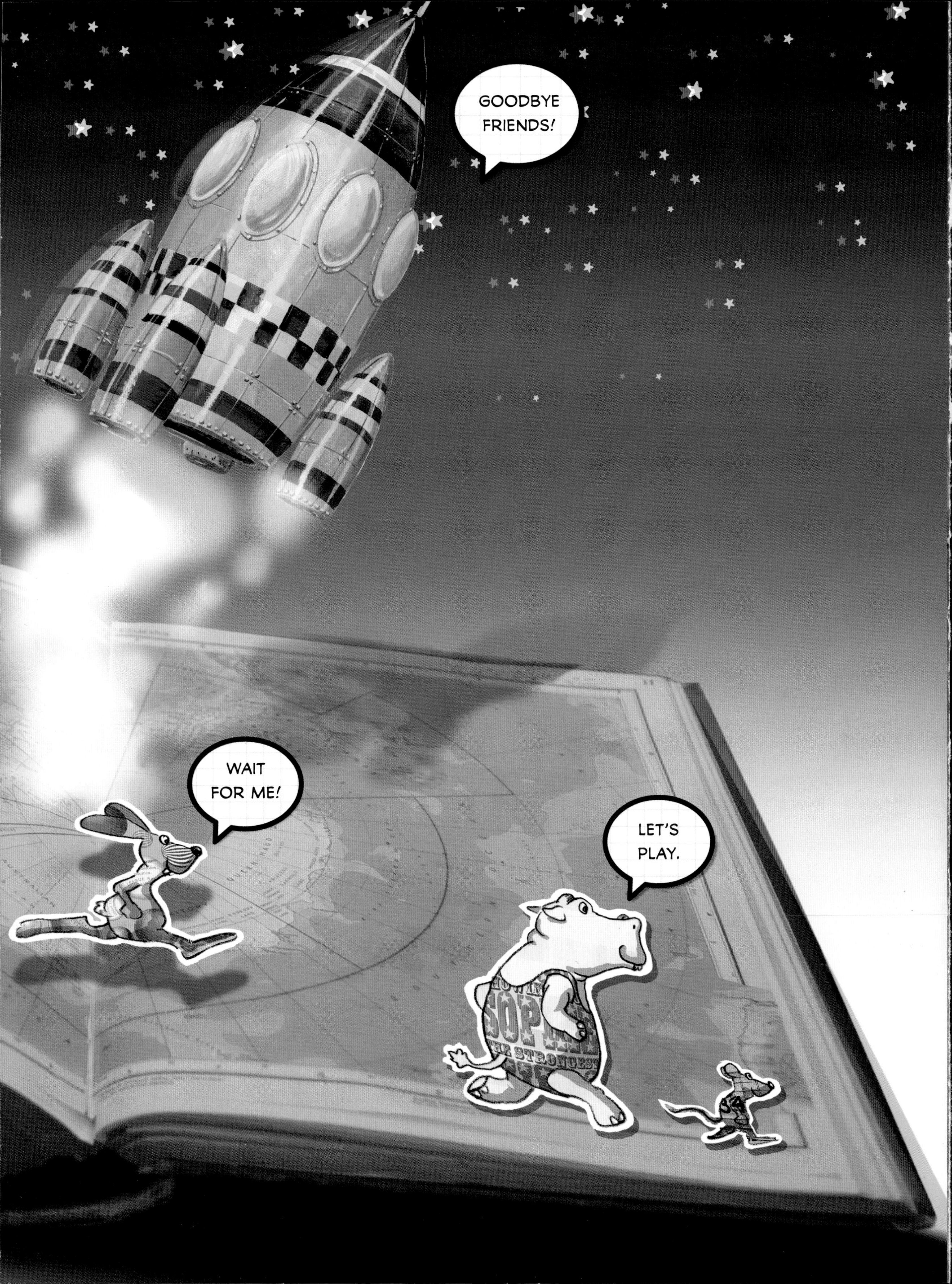
GOODBYE FRIENDS!
WAIT FOR ME!
LET'S PLAY.

... and it was even better than Ludwig had imagined.

Ludwig and the space explorer floated through space, past planets and stars . . .

Ludwig's friends often thought
about him when they played
their favourite games.

SPACE LAND

im Maßstand von 1 : 500000

And Ludwig sent them postcards,
with tales of his adventures from
another dimension.